TALES OF THE TEN COMMANDMENTS

50 FABLES TO HELP CHILDREN LEARN GOD'S LAW

JARED DEES

FORMATIVE FICTION

Scripture texts in this work are taken from the New Revised Standard Version Bible, copyright © 1989 the Division of Christian Education of the National Council of the Churches of Christ in the United States of America. Used by permission. All rights reserved.

© 2019 Jared Dees

All rights reserved.
No part of this book may be reproduced or used in any manner without written permission of the copyright owner except for the use of quotations in a book review.

For more information visit jareddees.com.

Paperback: ISBN 978-1-7332048-2-8
eBook: ISBN 978-1-7332048-3-5

First Edition

*For my students:
past, present, and future.*

CONTENTS

Introduction ix

THE FIRST COMMANDMENT

The Toy Dog 3
The Voice of the Song 5
The Broken Phone 7
The Inventor 11
The High School Graduate 13

THE SECOND COMMANDMENT

The Prayerful Parrot 17
The Self-Righteous Rabbit 19
The Missing Diary 21
The Song of Joy or Strife 23
The Disappointed Daughter 25

THE THIRD COMMANDMENT

The Funday 29
The Cuckoo Clock 31
The Worker Elves 33
The Day to Pray 35
The Hardworking Author 37

THE FOURTH COMMANDMENT

The Little Tree 41
The Boy with No Parents 43
The Football Player's Father 45
The Persistent Penguin 47
The Lion Cub 49

THE FIFTH COMMANDMENT

The Weed	53
The Toy Soldier	55
The Performer's Competitor	57
The Greedy Spider	61
The Ant Traps	63

THE SIXTH COMMANDMENT

The Two Tulips	67
The Beautiful Fox	69
The Stuffed Fish	71
The Jelly and the Peanut Butter	73
The Beavers' Dam	75

THE SEVENTH COMMANDMENT

The Princesses' Accessories	79
The Buried Treasure	81
The Hungry Mice	83
The Cheater	85
The Missing Socks	87

THE EIGHTH COMMANDMENT

The False Fox	91
The Tricky Chickens	93
The Honest Giraffe	95
The Lying Little Brother	97
The Gossiping Girl	99

THE NINTH COMMANDMENT

The Three Swans	103
The Pretend Husband	105
The Weed and the Flowers	107
The Tennis Shoe	109
The Old Wolves	111

THE TENTH COMMANDMENT

The Better Bike	115

The Computer and the Stickers	117
The Covetous Candlemaker	119
The Defenseless Rabbits	121
The Gamer	123
About the Author	125
Also by Jared Dees	127
Formative Fiction	129

INTRODUCTION

There is a country road near my childhood home with an unusually low speed limit. The distance between the Speed Limit 35 and Speed Limit 55 signs always seemed way too far. Nevertheless, when I got my driver's license, I knew never to break the speed limit on Bogart Road.

I had to drive along this road a lot, too. I worked as a pizza delivery driver during high school, and I had to use that road for deliveries. As all delivery drivers know, the faster you deliver the pizza, the faster you can get back to deliver more pizza. More deliveries meant more tips. I wanted to drive as fast as possible. I may have even broken the speed limit once or twice . . . but not on Bogart Road.

The dial on my dashboard pointed to 35 mph on the dot every time I drove along that road. Why? Because I knew that police officers often sat somewhere nearby, waiting to pull over speeding cars. I knew this because I had heard so many of my friends tell stories of getting pulled over and getting speeding tickets there.

This book exists to serve a very similar purpose. In it, you will find fifty fables and parables that warn of the consequences of breaking one of the Ten Commandments. I followed the speed limit on Bogart Road because of the stories I heard about people who got speeding tickets for driving too fast. I hope you will be inspired to follow the Ten Commandments with the help of these stories you read about people, animals, and objects that learn to follow God's law.

More than this, though, I hope these stories will also teach you about how to follow the Great Commandments. A lawyer once went up to Jesus and asked him, "Teacher, which commandment in the law is the greatest?" A lot of us might assume he meant which of the *Ten* Commandments is the greatest. But Jesus answered with Bible verses from two different places in the Old Testament: "You shall love the Lord your God with all your heart, and with all your strength, and with all your mind" (Dt 6:5). "This is the greatest and first commandment," he said, "And the second is like it: 'You shall love your neighbor as yourself' [Lv 19:18]" (see Mt 22:34–40).

What I love most about Jesus's answer is that these two greatest commandments actually summarize the Ten Commandments. In fact, the Ten Commandments simply explain in more detail how exactly we are to love God and love our neighbor. Let's categorize the Ten Commandments into two groups:

LOVE YOUR GOD

1. I am the LORD your God: you shall not have strange gods before me.
2. You shall not take the name of the LORD your God in vain.
3. Remember to keep holy the LORD's Day.

LOVE YOUR NEIGHBOR

4. Honor your father and your mother.
5. You shall not kill.
6. You shall not commit adultery.
7. You shall not steal.
8. You shall not bear false witness against your neighbor.
9. You shall not covet your neighbor's wife.
10. You shall not covet your neighbor's goods.

Do you see it? When we strive to follow the Ten Commandments, we are striving to love God and love our neighbor. This is about more than avoiding punishment.

If we break the speed limit while driving and get pulled over, then we will be punished with a speeding ticket and a fine to pay the city. That hurts. The pain is a good reason not to break the law. (For a pizza delivery driver, that fine would cost more than a week's worth of tips!)

When we break one of the Ten Commandments, however, the punishment is much more harsh, and we inflict it on ourselves. Breaking the Ten Commandments breaks the bond of love between us and God and between us and our neighbors. We hurt our relationship with God and others when we break the commandments.

Conversely, when we follow the Ten Commandments, we grow deeper in our loving relationship with God and with others. These commandments help us invite God to have an active presence in our lives. They allow us to be loved back by our parents, family, friends, and acquaintances. This not only makes us happy; it prevents us from ever having to feel alone.

When we apply the power of story to these commandments, with the fables and parables you are about to read, we can start to hear the words "you shall not" in a new way. We should certainly follow the commandments, because they are indeed God's laws. Beyond that, though, we can learn from those that have tried to break one of the commandments and the lessons they learned along the way, as well as those who have found greater peace and happiness in following them. May the lessons of the characters in this book become our lessons, and may we grow in the love of the Lord and each other as we follow God's Law.

THE FIRST COMMANDMENT

I am the LORD your God: you shall not have strange gods before me.

THE TOY DOG

There was a very furry toy dog in a young girl's bedroom. The girl loved her toy dog very much, but she also loved her real pet dog, too. The real dog had a lot of energy and loved to run and chase the girl around the house or throughout the backyard.

The toy dog also loved the real dog. He liked the girl, too, but he wished he belonged to the real dog rather than the girl. The real dog seemed to have so much more fun than its human owner.

One day, the real dog was left out of its cage and came into the girl's room where all the toys lived. The toys ran in fear of the real dog. They were afraid, but the toy dog wasn't. He loved the real dog and thought this was his chance to play with and be loved by the energetic animal.

He ran toward the dog in excitement. The real dog pounced on the toy dog and immediately began to chew on him.

The girl returned to her room to find her pet dog tearing the toy dog to pieces. She immediately began to cry and took her pet back to its cage.

She put the toy dog back together piece by piece,

sewing back on the arms and eyes that had been ripped off. He was never perfect again, but the girl loved him and repaired him anyway.

From that day on, the toy dog loved his human owner best. He did not love anyone or anything more than her forever.

I am the LORD your God: you shall not have strange gods before me.

THE VOICE OF THE SONG

A young musician dreamed of being famous someday. He practiced hard at his instruments and learned to play very well.

One day, he heard a voice in his head, calling him to sing a song he had never heard before. He wrote down the words and notes for the song and started to play it. Some people listening nearby heard the song and were amazed. They had to hear him play it again. He played it again for them and then to many other people afterward.

This song grew in popularity, and so did he. Everyone loved this young musician and the beautiful song he had created.

It wasn't long before he had to hire a manager to help him organize his shows and make more music. The manager had a lot of advice for the kinds of music the musician should write. He made many new songs based on these suggestions, but none of them earned as much attention as his original song. He sang and sang, but people stopped listening to him.

He went to other musicians and tried to get their advice. He listened to the many voices that told him to sing in many different ways. He tried many styles, but none of them earned him the love and admiration of his original song.

He went to his fans and asked them what they wanted to hear. They told him they didn't like his new songs. They only wanted to hear the one song they already loved.

All of the negative feedback made him want to quit making music. He thought back to the days before he was famous, when he first heard the voice that inspired that first, popular song.

Then it suddenly occurred to him. "The Voice!" he said. "Yes, the Voice! That is where the beautiful song came from. It didn't come from the manager or other musicians. It didn't come from my fans. It came from the Voice!

"Voice," he said looking up to the sky. "I don't know if you can hear me, but I'm sorry. I'm sorry I listened to everyone but you. It was you who inspired me all along. If you find me worthy, please give me another song to sing and share with the people of this world."

At first there was a dull silence. Then he heard the Voice again. It was giving him a song—a new song of joy and sorrow mixed together. This he wrote down, just as he had done years earlier. He played the song, and little by little, people came to hear him sing again. They loved the new song just as much as the first song.

The musician never listened to another voice again, and he never took credit for the creation of his art. It was the Voice's song all along.

I am the LORD your God: you shall not have strange gods before me.

THE BROKEN PHONE

There was a girl who became obsessed with her phone. She was constantly checking it to see if anyone had responded to her posts and text messages. It was the first thing she did every morning and the last thing she did every night.

She woke up one morning and picked up the phone beside her bed. It was turned off. She thought the battery must have died, but when she plugged it in, it wouldn't charge.

She immediately went to her parents. "Dad, my phone is broken! You have to fix it!"

"I'm sorry, honey, but it's the weekend, and there are too many things to do right now," said her father.

"But, Dad, I need that phone!" she protested.

"Leave it in the kitchen. I'll try to fix it later," he said.

The girl was devastated. She didn't know what to do. She couldn't communicate with anyone. She was completely isolated. All day long, she waited and begged her dad to fix the phone.

That night, her parents sat her down on the couch to talk to her.

"We're worried about you," said her mother. "You have become too attached to that phone. You've been on edge all day long, and we think it's time to take a break from the phone for a while."

"What? No way! I can't take a break," she said.

Her father pulled out a little book. It looked like the one he kept on his desk in his office.

"Try this," he said. "It's a journal. I write in it every morning."

"I don't want to keep some stupid diary!" she said. "I want my phone back!"

The parents kept calm, though they had every reason to be angry.

"It's not a diary," said her dad. "It's a conversation. It's a lot like your text messages, really. All I do is write a note to God. I talk to him by writing to him in my journal."

"We'll make a deal with you," said her mother. "You fill that journal up with conversations with God, and we will give you a new phone after the pages are filled."

The girl didn't like the idea, but she didn't want to waste any time, either. After their talk, she opened the journal and started to write. She wrote the whole night until she was too tired to write any more.

Before finally going to bed that night, she felt peaceful and calm—not like she usually felt before bed. She wasn't worried about a response to her posts or messages. She wasn't worried about being judged. She wasn't worried at all.

The next morning, she woke up, reached over to pick up her phone, and found the journal instead. She opened it up and started to write. Once again, she felt at peace. She could pour out her heart without any fear of being judged. She could write without worrying about the response.

At breakfast, she said to her parents, "Thanks for the

journal. I think I can go another day without the phone. I'll be just fine."

Her parents looked at one another and smiled. "We're very happy to hear that," said her father.

I am the LORD your God: you shall not have strange gods before me.

THE INVENTOR

There was an inventor who created many machines for every kind of problem. He was famous throughout the world for the many great things he created.

He was very happy and proud of his creations. He looked forward to making many more great inventions in the years ahead.

Then his wife became ill. She was very sick, and the doctors said that she had only a short time to live.

The inventor immediately went to work trying to make a machine to heal his wife. He worked many long hours and sleepless nights in his laboratory.

His wife, meanwhile, sat in bed alone, thinking and thanking God for the many great memories she had in her life with her family, friends, and husband, the inventor.

The husband worked harder and harder until, finally, he thought he had the answer. He thought he had a machine that could save her. He brought the machine home and took it up to his wife's bedroom.

There he found her on the brink of death. He had been away so long that he didn't realize how sick she had become.

He held her hand and sat by her side as she passed away.

The inventor picked up his machine and threw it against the wall. "Why, God, why?" he shouted.

To his surprise, God answered him. He heard the answer in his heart, "Trust in me."

The inventor was filled with an enormous sense of shame. He had spent the last days of his wife's life trusting in his own work rather than in God.

Next to his wife's bed, he found a letter that read:

My Dear Husband,
Thank you for our amazing life together. I am gone but not forgotten. Pray for me as I pray for you.
Love,
Your Adoring Wife

I am the LORD your God: you shall not have strange gods before me.

THE HIGH SCHOOL GRADUATE

After graduating high school, a young girl was going to college and had to decide what she wanted to be when she grew up. She wasn't sure what she should study, and she had to make a choice soon.

She went to her friends and asked them what they thought she should do after college. They were too worried about their own lives at other colleges to give her any good advice.

She went to her parents to ask them what she should be when she grew up. "You will figure it out," they said to reassure her. But she was still confused by all the different choices.

Then she turned to her favorite high school teacher for ideas. The teacher was honored to be asked for help. This teacher told her to search inside of herself for the answer.

She thought about this for a while after her conversation with the teacher, but she wasn't able to come up with any answers. She still didn't know what she should be when she grew up.

She decided to go to a church to pray. She knelt down and asked God for guidance. She turned to him for answers about what she was supposed to do with her life. She prayed and prayed but didn't hear an answer. She wasn't sure what she expected to hear, but she was hoping for something.

Then she ran into the priest of the church on her way out. She told him about her problem. She told him how she had turned to her friends, her family, and even her teachers before she ended up there in the church.

"You have come to the right place," said the priest.

"But God didn't give me an answer," said the girl.

"And neither did your friends or family or teachers, correct?" he asked.

"Yes, what am I supposed to do?" she asked.

The priest smiled. "Well, I don't know, either, but I do know one thing. There is only one who you turned to that will be with you as you continue to search. Your friends will go off and lead new lives. Your family will remain here. Your teachers will teach new children each year. But only God will be by your side as you go on to college."

"But he didn't give me an answer," she said.

"Not yet, but I suspect he will when you least expect it," said the priest.

Weeks later, the girl went off to college. She studied hard and changed her mind often about what she wanted to study. Throughout all this time, though, she turned to God in prayer to help her make the right decisions. She felt an inner peace about the decisions she made, and when she graduated college years later, she started a wonderful career that she knew God had called her to.

I am the LORD your God: you shall not have strange gods before me.

THE SECOND COMMANDMENT

You shall not take the name of the LORD your God in vain.

THE PRAYERFUL PARROT

A family had a pet parrot who only knew a few words. One of those words was "Jesus."

For a while, the parrot responded with the word "Jesus" to almost anything people said to him, so the kids in the house thought it would be funny to ask him silly questions.

"What's your name?" they asked the bird.

"Awk. Jesus. Awk," replied the bird.

The kids giggled at the answer.

One of the boys punched his brother. Then he asked the parrot, "Who did that?"

"Jesus," said the bird, and the boy roared with laughter.

The brother didn't like that so much. He said to the bird, "Who hates my brother even more than me?"

"Jesus," said the bird.

These kinds of mean questions continued for a while longer.

Then the mother of the family came in and heard what was going on, and it made her angry. "That is quite enough," she said to them.

She thought about punishing the boys, but she decided to teach them a lesson instead.

"Parrot, who created us?" she asked.

"Jesus," said the bird.

"And who saves us?" she asked.

"Jesus," he said again.

"And who watches over us when we need help?"

"Jesus."

"And who forgives us no matter how badly we hurt him?"

"Jesus."

"Boys, I think you have some praying to do," the mother said to her sons. "The name of the Lord is no laughing matter."

"Yes, Mom," said the brothers.

"Sorry," said the older brother.

"Yeah, sorry," said the younger brother.

"Don't say sorry to me," said their mother.

"Sorry, parrot," said the younger of the boys.

"Sorry, God," said the other, looking up to the sky.

"Awk. Amen. Awk," said the bird.

You shall not take the name of the LORD your God in vain.

THE SELF-RIGHTEOUS RABBIT

There were so many rabbits living in a field that the homes within their holes started to be very crowded. Things were starting to get uncomfortable, and one day, a very cunning rabbit had an idea.

In the middle of the field stood a very tall tree with a rabbit hole below it that all the rabbits shared as a place where they could gather and rest together. It was the most spacious hole in the field. The cunning rabbit jumped up onto a low-hanging branch from the tree. This was a very odd thing for a rabbit to do, and the others looked at him in wonder.

The rabbit on the branch stared up into the tree. "My fellow rabbits," he said. "I see the Lord God in the tree. He is speaking to me! He says that I am a special chosen rabbit. I am to take residence in the hole below this tree and guard it as a holy place. I am to live here alone, with no other rabbits."

The other rabbits looked at one another in fear. Something like this had never happened before. The rabbit in the tree hopped down and into the large hole all by himself. Inside, he felt very pleased with himself and the lie he had told about God.

Whenever he came out of the hole to find food or have fun, he would say, "I come in the name of the Lord!" The other rabbits wanted to please God, so they did everything they could to make him happy and comfortable.

This went on for weeks, until this rabbit ran into a groundhog in another part of the field. The groundhog was bragging about the spacious size of his underground home.

"Well, you should see my home!" said the rabbit. "It was made for many other rabbits, but I tricked them all into thinking it was just for me. I told them it was God's will that I have the hole all to myself, and they believed me! Ha!"

A few other rabbits were nibbling on grass behind a nearby bush and overheard what the rabbit said to the groundhog. They ran quickly back toward the tree in the middle of the field, telling all the other rabbits what they had heard.

When the cunning rabbit returned to the hole below the tree, he found it full of rabbits.

"But the Lord has said this hole is for me alone!" said the rabbit.

"We heard what you said to the groundhog. Your pride has gotten the best of you. This hole is for all rabbits to share."

"But not for you," said one particularly large rabbit, who pushed him back out of the hole.

The rabbit was never allowed to return to the common hole and the others never believed anything that rabbit said again.

You shall not take the name of the LORD your God in vain.

THE MISSING DIARY

The youngest brother in a family sneaked into his sister's room and found her diary. He found it funny to read her secret thoughts.

But one day, his sister found him in her room. He quickly shoved the diary under her bed.

"What are you doing in here?" she asked him.

"Nothing!" he said as he ran back to his room.

A few minutes later, his sister was in his room with her arms crossed and an angry expression on her face.

"Where is my diary? Do you have it? Did you read it?" she asked angrily.

"No!" said the boy.

The girl narrowed her eyes. "Swear it. Swear to God you didn't read it," she said to him.

The boy hesitated, but he didn't want to get caught. "I swear it."

"Swear to God?" she asked.

"I swear to God I didn't read your diary," said the boy.

His sister turned and left him.

The boy had lied, but worse than that, he swore to God when he lied. At first it didn't bother him. She would find the diary eventually. But then the guilt really started to set in.

And then the fear came, too. What would God think of him for lying like this?

He went back to his sister's room. The room was a mess from her search.

"It's under your bed," said the brother. "I'm sorry."

"Ugh, I can't believe you! Did you read it?" she asked again.

"No!" said the boy.

"Do you swear to God?" his sister asked him.

The boy couldn't lie to her and to God again. He looked down. "Okay, I did read it. I'm sorry."

She was furious. "Get out!" she said.

The boy left his sister's room. He paused and closed his eyes. "I'm sorry to you, too, God," he said in prayer. "I hope you will forgive me."

He felt peace and knew that God would forgive him.

His sister didn't talk to him for a few days after that, but eventually she forgave him, too.

You shall not take the name of the LORD your God in vain.

THE SONG OF JOY OR STRIFE

A magical musician lived in a cabin alone in the woods. There, he composed many songs that did many magical things. He crafted his songs in a secluded place because the magic of music was very hard to control.

One day, a traveler passed and heard some beautiful music coming from the magical musician's home. He peeked into the window and listened to the music. Soon, he learned the tune and walked away, whistling it to himself.

Now, this particular song had a very powerful magic in it. When sung for the good of others, it filled the singer and the audience with joy. This is why the traveler was so interested in the song in the first place. However, when sung to attract the affection or admiration of others, this song brought hatred and strife between people.

When the traveler arrived in the nearby town, he saw a sad old man sitting in the street. He sang the song for the man, and they both were filled with hope and joy.

The traveler felt happy, but he made the mistake of thinking that it was his ability to sing the song that brought the joy, rather than the song itself.

From there, he saw others in the streets and started to sing this song for them, hoping to earn their affection and appreciation for his music. Instead, the people became angry with the traveler and then angry with each other and everyone else they met.

The song was repeated from person to person, not to spread joy but to show each other that they were the better singers of the song. More and more, they competed and hated one another.

The next day, the musician from the woods came into town to buy supplies. There, he heard his song being sung in vain. It was sung with selfishness, with many people trying to out-sing one another.

This was not the way of the song. The musician knew that humility was essential for the song to spread joy.

The magical musician sang his tune in the back alleys and hidden places of the town, inspiring joy and appreciation for the song itself and not for the singer. In that way, he brought joy back into the hearts of the townspeople.

He met the traveler on the road outside the town. The man was now forlorn and no longer singing.

"Let me give you a new song," the musician said to the traveler. "It is only one word: Alleluia. Sing this song and this word with a full heart, and the joy of this life will never be lost."

You shall not take the name of the LORD your God in vain.

THE DISAPPOINTED DAUGHTER

A girl loved to work on projects around the house with her father in the evenings and on the weekends. She liked spending time with him and learning from him. But there was one thing that she didn't like. When he was really angry or hurt himself, he would curse in the name of Jesus.

Every time he did it, the daughter winced as if in pain. She knew it was wrong, and she didn't like hearing it from her father, whom she loved.

One day, they were working with a hammer and nails, and he accidentally hit his thumb with the hammer. He cursed in Jesus' name immediately.

"Dad," she said. "Can you say something else besides Jesus' name when you get angry? It really bothers me."

The father was still in pain. "Oh c'mon," he said. "I can't help what I say when I get hurt like that. What's the big deal?"

The daughter was sad, but she didn't say anything to argue with him. He was her father, after all.

He cursed in Jesus' name once more that day and saw how sad it made his daughter feel. Later that day, he went to tuck her into bed. She was kneeling beside her bed and praying, "Jesus, please forgive him for saying those things. It's just a habit. He doesn't really mean it."

The father was ashamed. Bad habit or not, it was something he now wanted to change. From that day forward, he tried his best to bite his tongue rather than curse in the name of the Lord. This made his daughter very happy and very proud of him.

You shall not take the name of the LORD your God in vain.

THE THIRD COMMANDMENT

Remember to keep holy the LORD's Day.

THE FUNDAY

There was a girl who thought Sundays were too boring. She decided to rename Sunday as "Funday."

"Funday is going to be the best," she told her mom. "I will do whatever I want. I will wake up late and eat candy for breakfast. I will watch movies and sit on the couch. I will play video games on my iPad. I will play outside with my friends. I won't do any chores, and I definitely won't go to boring old church in the morning."

"Is that so?" said the mother. At first she laughed, knowing that this was simply out of the question. Then she thought this might be an opportunity to teach a lesson.

"Okay," she said to her daughter. "Try it, and let's see how it goes."

The next Sunday, the family woke up to go to church. The daughter stayed home and ate candy for breakfast while watching one of her favorite movies.

The movie ended and her family still wasn't home. She made herself some lunch (a Nutella sandwich with marshmallows and gummy bears on the side) and put another movie in.

Finally, the family arrived home in the afternoon. "How is your day going, sweetheart?" the mother asked.

The girl was tired and feeling a little sick from all the sugar, but she said, "Lots of fun!"

She didn't really mean it. It wasn't very fun being all alone and not getting to share the day with her family.

"Well, enjoy it," said the mother. "We went to lunch after church, and now we are heading back for games and a picnic dinner there with a bunch of other families. We will see you later."

The girl wasn't having any fun at all. Now she thought of all the fun people she knew at church. She thought of how church, even though it was sometimes boring, made her feel good about herself when she left. Here at home, alone, she just felt sick and sad for not really doing anything all day.

"I declare Funday to be over. Sunday has now returned!" the girl shouted.

The girl went to church with her mom after the picnic that day, and she never missed church on Sunday again.

Remember to keep holy the LORD's Day.

THE CUCKOO CLOCK

Every day, a plastic blue bird announced the turning of its clock with a high-pitched, "Cuckoo, cuckoo." Day after day, the bird never missed an hour. It was dedicated to its work. This was its duty.

The clock with the blue bird became a family heirloom, passed on from one generation to the next. At each new home, the cuckoo never stopped.

One day, the little bird saw another kind of clock in the house. It was an alarm clock. Rather than a big hand and a little hand traveling around in circles, this clock had only numbers. It made a sound only once each morning. It did not cuckoo or beep every hour.

One day, after the people in the house had left, the cuckoo peeked out of the doors and said to the other clock, "Clock, how do you remain so silent all the time?"

The numbers on the clock blinked like eyes, and then it spoke. "I am an alarm clock, little bird."

"Why do you not work as hard as I do, announcing the new hour every day?" asked the bird.

"I give our owner rest in the night," said the clock.

"Why would you prefer rest over work?" asked the bird.

"Rest is not inaction. Rest is a chance to find alignment. Let me ask you, birdie: why do you announce the hour even when no one is around to hear?"

The bird thought for a moment, then said, "It is my job."

"What would happen if you set aside this hour for rest rather than work? What would happen?"

"I could never!" said the bird.

"Try it," said the clock.

The bird went back into its doors and waited. It had never missed an hour in all its life. This was its duty. This was its purpose. It had to work, work, work and never make a mistake.

What would happen? The bird heard the clock strike noon, and no one was around. The doors opened, but the bird remained inside.

The next hour was a thoughtful one. He appreciated his work so much more now that he had had a chance to rest.

The hour struck again, and this time the birdie came out with a renewed sense of joy and purpose. "Cuckoo!" it cried with a spirit of joy that it hadn't felt in years. "Cuckoo!" it cried, announcing a new hour and a new moment to live out the purpose each one of us was sent here to achieve.

Remember to keep holy the LORD's Day.

THE WORKER ELVES

In a magical kingdom, there were many worker elves who served the king of the land with pride. They were loyal servants and wanted nothing more than to make the king happy. They were a merry bunch, too, always smiling and full of joy. They worked very hard and for many hours, but they only worked every other day. On their off days, they spent time together with friends and family and gave thanks for their happy lives.

Then one day, the king died, and his greedy son was crowned in his place.

The new king had always resented the elves for smiling all the time. He felt they should work every day and help make the kingdom richer than any other kingdom of the land.

The king declared an edict that all elves should work every day, not every other day, from that moment forward.

The elves were loyal and obeyed without complaint. They worked harder than ever and longer than ever. They never tired. It seemed to the king that this was a great decision and he would be very, very rich before long.

Indeed, he was right, at first. His kingdom did grow in riches and did become the richest of the land.

The elves never seemed to get tired. They worked so hard each and every day.

But as the kingdom got richer, the elves got angrier. They worked hard, but they resented the work. They started to hate the work and the king. They even grew angry with each other. Many fights broke out between the elves. Without their days off, they never had time to spend with one another. They accused each other of stealing or not working hard enough. They tried to outwork and be better than one another, all the while hating anyone that tried to compete with them.

The king didn't notice or care. He was happy with all his new riches. He didn't expect what would happen next.

The elves had grown so angry that each one thought he should be king instead. They went after the king to capture and overthrow him.

The castle guard stopped the elves and protected the king, but the elves would never work for him again. They all saw themselves as better than each other and better than the king.

After quitting and having some time away from work, however, they grew to enjoy each other once more. They spent time with one another, and together they traveled to a new kingdom to serve a new king. The old king was left with nothing to make him rich or happy.

Remember to keep holy the LORD's Day.

THE DAY TO PRAY

The farmers of a small kingdom were very far behind in harvesting their crops. The king was worried that there would not be enough food collected for the people to store for the winter.

The king knew that the farmers worked six days out of the week but customarily rested on the seventh day. He decided that the best thing to do would be to ban this day of rest. The king thought the crisis called for desperate measures. The farmers must work harder and never rest until the crops were harvested.

When the people heard the proclamation, they marched to the castle in opposition. There was a very angry mob waiting for the king to answer for his ban of the day of rest.

The king came to the balcony to speak to the people. "Dear farmers, why do you oppose this decision? We must harvest the crops, and quickly, if you are to avoid hunger in the winter months."

"We must have our day of rest!" they objected.

The king thought they were upset because they were

tired. He thought they just wanted a break from all the hard work.

"It is only for a short time. Work harder, and we can restore the resting day later," he shouted.

One of the leaders of the group stepped forward and said, "Dear King, the day is about more than rest from work. We are tired, yes, but that is not why we need this day."

The king was confused. Was he so far out of touch with the reasons his subjects did what they did?

"It is a day we set aside not for ourselves, but for God! It is a day we pray. This may seem like a break, but it is not a day for laziness."

The king was curious about this. The leader of the farmers went on.

"For who helps the crops grow? Who gives us such great food to eat? Who else but God, who made us?" said the farmer.

The king realized his error. He had been so worried for his people that he forgot the true purpose of the day of rest. It was not a day to be lazy but a day to pray and thank God for all his good gifts. He didn't have to think long about changing his mind.

"Very well! I relinquish the ban. Take your day to rest and pray. We will place our trust in God rather than your hard work alone to save us."

The farmers were right. They did take their days to rest and pray, and there was plenty of food for the winter months. God provided more than enough, and the people were very grateful.

Remember to keep holy the LORD's Day.

THE HARDWORKING AUTHOR

There was an author who wanted to inspire the people of the world to be filled with joy and happiness. He was a faithful person, and so he wanted to write his next book about having a relationship with God. He dreamed about all the people he could inspire with this book.

He stocked up on food and determined to write feverishly every day of the week until he finished his book.

On Monday, he sat down to write. It was hard, but he made a lot of progress, beginning in the morning and ending at night.

Tuesday through Friday was about the same. He had times when it was difficult to write, but he pushed through and made great progress on his book.

When the weekend came, he didn't slow down. On Saturday, he wrote more than any of the other days of the week thus far. He was proud of himself and eager to finish the work so others could read it and tell him how good it was.

On Sunday, he woke up early and got right back to work. He worked straight through the day without stopping, so he could finish the book. In the evening on

Sunday, he finished. He was very tired but very proud. He was sure this book would become a bestseller.

On Monday, he showed the book to some of his writer friends. They read some of it, and the author was eager to hear their praise for his work.

Instead, each one looked a little confused.

"What is it?" asked the author.

"Well, what is your book about?" they asked.

"It is about life, God, love, and faith!" said the author.

There was a silent pause. One of his friends said, "Well, I hate to say this, but I think the story is really only about you. If it's about God, then I have to ask: did you pray at all during the writing of this book?"

"Well, no," he said. "I had too much work to do and so little time."

"Did you take some time off on Sunday, at least, to think about God?" asked another friend.

"Well, no, but I needed to finish it!" he replied.

The friends were not impressed, and the author realized that they were right. He had worked hard and had finished the book, but it was uninspired and more about him than God. If he had taken some time on Sunday to think and pray about this, then he might have been able to make it better.

Remember to keep holy the LORD's Day.

THE FOURTH COMMANDMENT

Honor your father and your mother.

THE LITTLE TREE

A seed fell from a very large tree and landed in the ground. It sprouted and grew to become a small tree in the shade of its parent tree.

This little tree grew bit by bit but never very quickly, and it did not become very large.

The little tree resented this and blamed its parent tree, saying, "I am always in your shadow and never able to grow great and strong. I wish I was far away from you so that I could grow large—even larger than you."

This greatly saddened the parent tree. "My little one, I have always cared for you and helped you grow. You must trust me."

"Little one? Must I grow in your shadow and stay so small for all my days?"

At that moment, something incredible happened. The little tree got its wish. A great and terrible earthquake split the ground between the two trees. A great chasm separated them, and the little tree no longer grew in the shadow of the parent tree.

Now the little tree could see the parent tree in its entirety. Above the recognizable underbrush that it knew so well was a layer of charred gray branches. This tree was great, indeed, but at its top it was mangled and burned from the sun.

That's when the little tree felt the heat of the sun for the first time. The leaves at its top quickly withered, as did the branches that held them.

This forever stunted the growth of the little tree. It remained little and at a distance so great from its parent that it was never able to say how sorry it was for the words that it had said before they were separated.

The little tree wished it had trusted its parent and stayed safe in the loving shadow of its branches.

Honor your father and your mother.

THE BOY WITH NO PARENTS

There was a young boy who lived in a big house. The only other people there were the servants and workers who maintained the property. No one ever saw the boy's parents.

The boy was quiet. He liked to come and play with the other kids in the town, but inevitably, they would ask about his parents. This just made the boy sad. He never explained what had happened to them.

The other kids started to make up stories about the missing parents. Some said they were thieves who were sent to jail. Others said that they didn't like the boy and just left him home to go and travel the world.

The boy never responded to the rumors. They just made him sad.

On one particular day, a gang of larger boys stood outside the gate of the large home, talking to each other. The boy came out of the home, walked through the gate, and walked down the road. The larger boys followed him.

"Hey, kid," they said. "Where's your mom and dad?"

The boy just kept walking.

"Hey, kid, we're talking to you!"

The boy didn't say a word.

"Where you going, boy? Are you heading to the jail to see Daddy?"

No answer.

"Nah. His parents aren't here. They left him a long time ago. They don't love him."

Still, the boy remained silent.

"I'm glad I don't have parents like that," said one of the boys. "My parents love me."

The kids laughed. The boy stopped. He turned and stared at the boys. Eventually, they stopped laughing. The boy didn't stop glaring at them.

Finally, he spoke. "Follow me," he said.

The boys broke out in laughter, but they followed him anyway. They continued to make jokes and tell stories about the boy's parents as they followed behind.

Finally, the boy stopped walking. Next to him was another gate, similar to the one near the boy's house.

He opened the gate and motioned for the others to follow.

It was at this time that the other boys realized what the boy was holding. He had two flowers in his hands.

The boy walked to the top of a hill and stopped. The other kids arrived shortly after him.

The boy looked down, and tears were in his eyes. He laid the two flowers upon his parents' shared tombstone. Inscribed under their names were the words:

"Who loved their son very much."

Honor your father and your mother.

THE FOOTBALL PLAYER'S FATHER

A famous football player stood before a room of people for the pregame press conference. It was his last game before retirement. People loved him, but not as much as they loved his father. His father had been a great football player, too, and some called him the greatest of all time.

"Do you think you lived up to your dad's legacy?" one reporter asked.

"Would your dad be proud of you?" asked another.

Question after question came in, asking about the player's dad and not him. This was the player's last game. He had a very accomplished career of his own. He had a lot to celebrate.

And yet, during his entire career, he was always compared to his father. He was always told that he wasn't as good as his dad. He had every reason to be angry with these reporters, who did not even congratulate him on his own great career.

Instead, this football player did what he had done his entire life. He responded confidently, "If I could achieve even a small amount of my father's success, then I will have led a great career. I will always look to him with respect and admiration. Thank you for asking about him."

Honor your father and your mother.

THE PERSISTENT PENGUIN

There was a penguin unlike the many other penguins in his clan. He wanted to explore the world, but the other penguins knew this was impossible. They needed to stay behind each winter and join together to care for the young and keep the eggs warm.

The weather was getting colder. It was time to join together in the pack to keep warm and protect the eggs. They huddled together and prepared for the winter.

Except the one penguin. He longed to go off alone. He was desperate to explore and about to set off on his own when his brother came to speak with him.

"You should not go," said the brother.

"But look at the great world out there!" replied the penguin. "It is just meant to be explored."

"You will die," said his brother.

"You don't know that," said the penguin.

"True, but the chances of survival are slim," he said.

"It is worth the risk. How can I stay here when there is so much to explore?"

The brother thought for a moment and said, "You are here because of our parents. Our father kept us warm in the winter. You must do the same for the rest of our penguin cousins and neighbors."

The penguin thought for a moment. He loved his parents and appreciated the sacrifices they had made for him. While he did not have a mate yet and had no egg of his own to care for that winter, he knew the other penguins needed him to help keep each other warm.

"Stay to honor what they did for you," said his brother.

So the penguin did. He stayed through the winter, helping the other penguins. He stayed the following year, too, and in time, he found a mate and cared for a penguin egg of his own with the help of the other penguins.

Honor your father and your mother.

THE LION CUB

A little lion cub rarely saw his father, who was always out hunting and rarely home with the cub's mother. The more the father was away, the less the lion cub liked him.

The father lion came back to their den one day, but the cub fled as soon as he saw him. He didn't want to be around his father, who was never there. This made the father angry, but the mother lion went out to speak with her son.

"Why do you flee from your father like that?" she asked.

"He's never here. Why should I be around him if he doesn't want to be around us?" the cub asked.

The mother lion looked down on her son. "He is your father. Whether he is here often or a little, he is still your father. Cherish the time he is here, because he spends the rest of the day hunting for food for our family."

The cub was still upset, but he always listened to his mother. He returned to the den and apologized to his father. Then he asked him to share stories about his adventures on the hunt. At first, the father didn't want to talk. He just wanted to rest, but the cub was persistent, and so he started to talk. The father started to tell stories about his lion adventures out on the hunt.

When he finished telling the stories, the lion cub asked, "Can I go with you sometime?"

The father smiled and thought for a moment. "Yes, someday we will go out together, and then we will return and share stories about the new adventures we make together."

Honor your father and your mother.

THE FIFTH COMMANDMENT

You shall not kill.

THE WEED

A weed grew in a garden full of vegetables. The weed saw how much the farmer loved the vegetables, and the weed hated them.

The weed grew so it could overcome the other plants. It intertwined its vines and established the roots of new weeds to take the water and sun away from the vegetables. These weeds grew throughout the garden, and the vegetables stopped growing.

The farmer returned. He saw the weeds and was shocked at how fast they had grown. He took a shovel and a knife and cut the roots of all the weeds in the garden out of the soil. Then he piled them up to be burned.

Meanwhile, there were other weeds in the fields outside of the garden. They grew alone without any food-bearing plants around them. They looked at the weeds in the garden and felt pity for them.

The weeds in the fields grew freely and avoided vegetable plants. They found other places to get their sun and water. The farmer never bothered them at all.

You shall not kill.

THE TOY SOLDIER

There was a toy soldier who had a mission: kill the laughing bear.

There were reports from the other toys that this animal was laughing at all of them. It was laughing hysterically, and the other toys couldn't take it anymore. It was unbearable, and the other toys felt bad about themselves around him. So they turned to the head army man, the last remaining special ops soldier.

The army man accepted this mission and set out to stop the laughing bear. His goal was to remove the batteries from the bear's foot to silence him.

The soldier could hear the laughing from the other end of the bedroom. He climbed out of the toy chest, jumping down into a pile of clothes next to the bed.

Quietly, he inched closer and closer to the laughing bear.

In his hands, he had replaced the plastic gun he usually carried with a small screwdriver he had borrowed from the kitchen the night before. It was heavy, but it was the only way to remove the battery panel from the foot of the bear.

The laughing got louder and louder as he approached.

He saw the sadness in the faces of the other toys nearby. It was painful for them to hear, and they all felt like he was laughing right at them.

The soldier tied the end of a yo-yo rope onto the screwdriver, tossed the yo-yo over the bedframe, and caught it on the other side. He pulled himself and the screwdriver up to the bedpost, untied the knot, and took the screwdriver with him toward the bear.

Then a young boy arrived in the bedroom. It was the toys' owner.

The boy jumped onto the bed, nearly launching the soldier back to the floor. Luckily, the soldier grabbed the blanket just in time and held on. He pulled himself and the screwdriver back up to the bed and lay completely still.

That's when he saw them: the boy and the bear.

The boy was smiling. He was laughing. The bear was laughing, too. They were not laughing at anyone or anything. They were just happy.

The soldier remembered that the boy had saved him years ago from being melted like the other soldiers. This soldier was the last survivor, and he had the toys' owner to thank. The soldier loved the owner, and he could see that the bear loved the boy, too.

His determination to kill the bear turned to a smirk, then a smile, then full laughter. Anyone that the owner loved was worth the love of the soldier, too.

The toy soldier returned to the toy chest to report what he saw. He explained that the bear was laughing because of his love for the boy. The toys felt very bad for what they wanted to do. They never asked the soldier to hurt another toy again, and the soldier never did.

You shall not kill.

THE PERFORMER'S COMPETITOR

There once was a traveling performer who loved putting on shows for crowds of people. He was beloved for his funny shows.

One day, he arrived in town to find another performer setting up a similar show. He didn't pay much heed at first, until much of his audience left to go see his competitor, instead.

So he went to the next town, and the same thing happened. The people went to see the other show, and his own audience was nearly empty.

His crowds became smaller and smaller at each town, while the other performer's crowds were larger and larger. Everywhere he went, the first performer could not escape his competitor.

He felt he had to do something about this new performer. He used to be the only performer in the towns and got all the attention. Now he barely had an audience at all.

As he was thinking about ways to get rid of his competitor, he put on a show in a small town. As in the other towns, the audience was sparse. In fact, there was only one person in the audience—someone in dark robes, whose face was mostly hidden.

"Thank you for staying," the performer said to the one person in his audience, once he had completed his show.

"You deserve a larger audience," the mysterious person said to the performer.

"They all went to see my competition," he said bitterly.

"Yes, I know. What if your competition was gone? What would happen then?"

"Well, I guess they would come to see me instead," he replied.

"Is it your wish for this to be done?" the dark figure asked.

The performer thought for a moment, then replied, "Yes, but how could that be possible?"

The dark figure disappeared in a cloud of smoke.

Frightened by the exchange, the performer packed up his things and went on to the next town.

There, he heard the news about his competitor, who had disappeared during his performance in a cloud of dark smoke. The audience all thought it was a part of the show, but he never came back.

The many people in the land told stories about the missing performer and his shows. They loved those shows and missed him.

The first performer was sad for the competitor but glad that his audiences would be returning. He set up for the next show and got up onstage to find the audience just as empty as before.

He went searching for the people, and he soon found them gathered together, recreating the shows of his competitor as impersonators. Soon the competitor's show was recreated by many others throughout the land. These shows grew and grew in popularity.

The audiences never came back to see the first performer. They were more interested in the memory of his competition than attending his shows.

You shall not kill.

THE GREEDY SPIDER

A spider spent most of its life catching and eating only enough bugs to keep itself from starving. Day after day, the spider slowly caught the few flies it needed to survive.

Then one day, it decided that it wanted to catch more than it needed. This idea made it feel powerful. It felt confident in its ability to catch every fly in the whole house.

The spider built a great web—larger than any web it had ever built before. Then it waited.

Fly after fly was caught in the web. Other insects were caught in the web, too. The spider looked with pride at the great web and the large number of captures.

The spider moved along the web, trying to decide which fly to eat first. It wanted to kill not so it could satisfy its hunger, but so it could keep them from getting away.

As the spider moved its way toward the bottom of the web to make its first kill, the web broke. The web was too heavy with all the other bugs to hold the weight of the spider. It fell a very long distance, and the spider fell to its own death.

You shall not kill.

THE ANT TRAPS

A young boy saw his mother putting out ant traps in their yard. They were just boring traps from the store. He thought he could make something more fun to kill the ants.

He built water traps to drown the ants and got a magnifying glass to burn them with the sun's rays. He laughed as he watched them drown and burn.

"What are you doing?" asked his mother.

The boy looked up. "Killing ants!" he replied.

"Why are you torturing them like that?" she asked.

The boy was confused. "What do you mean? They're just ants."

"Whether they are ants or animals, we should not kill them like this. We should not take pleasure in inflicting pain on anyone or anything," she explained.

"But you set out ant traps to kill them," he pointed out.

"Yes, I set out traps to protect our house and our garden. I set out traps so the ants wouldn't overrun our yard," she said.

"But isn't that the same thing?" asked the boy.

"My traps will kill the ants, but I don't take pleasure in killing them. I do not torture them and hurt them for fun. I do it because we have to. There's a big difference," said the mom.

The boy put down his magnifying glass and gathered up his other traps. He helped his mom set out a few more of the store traps to stop the ants from coming in the house, but he did not torture them anymore.

You shall not kill.

THE SIXTH COMMANDMENT

You shall not commit adultery.

THE TWO TULIPS

Two tulips grew in a pot together. There was a yellow tulip and a red tulip. They had a great life and were very happy together, until one day a pot with a red rose was placed next to them.

The red tulip was very interested in this new red flower growing beside them. It turned away from the yellow tulip and leaned toward the red rose instead.

It leaned and stretched as far as it could reach and finally touched the red rose.

The yellow tulip felt hurt and alone. But it stood tall and strong, even though it felt awful about being left by the red tulip.

The red tulip tried to stretch and lean even farther, to get closer to the red rose, but after all the reaching and leaning, the red tulip snapped at the root. It was broken and had to be removed from the pot, never to grow again —neither with the yellow tulip nor the red rose.

You shall not commit adultery.

THE BEAUTIFUL FOX

A beautiful fox went strolling through the forest one day. Animals of all kinds came to see her and admire her beauty. Many of the other animals watched the fox so closely that they forgot about their own wives.

Animal after animal came to see her. One male hare left his home and his wife to see the beautiful fox a little closer. He walked right up to her and stood in her path.

The fox grinned and said, "Why, little rabbit, you have let your eyes get the best of you. What you longed to see up close will now devour you."

The fox flashed her fangs at the rabbit and leaped toward him. The rabbit ducked under the fox, but she still took a bite out of his ear. The rabbit ran, and the fox followed as long as she could. Eventually, the rabbit got away and returned home.

The rabbit's ear was red with blood, and his heart was heavy with guilt. He told his wife everything that had happened. She was very disappointed in him, but happy he was alive.

You shall not commit adultery.

THE STUFFED FISH

There was a stuffed animal fish that lived in her owner's bed with a stuffed teddy bear. She loved the teddy bear, and he loved her, too, but as a fish, she often felt she wanted to be with the water toys in the bathroom instead of in the bedroom.

The owner let the bath toys swim in real water. They sounded amazing, splashing in the water and swimming around at bath time. The stuffed fish longed to be with those bathtub fish.

The owner had a little brother who loved to take the bedroom toys out of the owner's room. He came in one day, throwing the animals off the bed. Then he saw the stuffed fish. "Fishy-fishy," he said, then, "Bath-bath."

He took the soft fish and toddled into the bathroom, throwing her in the bathtub with the other bath toys.

The stuffed fish was elated. She was finally with the other bath toys instead of in the bedroom.

She watched the other bath fish lying there and couldn't wait to swim with them. She never swam in real water.

Finally, her moment came. The owner's mother turned

on the bath water without paying attention to which toys were in the tub.

The water rose and rose, but the stuffed fish didn't float. She sunk lower and lower and filled with water. She was supposed to be swimming with the other fish, but instead, she was sinking.

"Honey, I gave the kids a bath last night. They are probably good for another day," said the owner's dad.

"Oh, okay," the mother responded and turned the water off.

The water drained out of the tub, but not out of the soft fish. She was now stuffed with cotton and with water.

The other fish in the bath stared at her, knowing that she had done something wrong. She didn't belong there.

She sat in the bath stuffed with water all night and into the next day. She began to smell. She smelled very bad by the time the mother returned the next night.

"Oh, no," said the mother. "What are you doing here?"

The mother picked the fish up and squeezed the water out of her. Then she took her to the laundry room to be washed.

The washing machine and the dryer tossed the fish around violently in circles. When the mother pulled the fish out of the dryer, it was hardly stuffed at all. Now it was more flat than fluffy.

When the mother returned the fish to the bed, the teddy bear was crying. He missed the fish and felt hurt that she had left him. It was very hard to welcome her back.

You shall not commit adultery.

THE JELLY AND THE PEANUT BUTTER

Together, the peanut butter and the jelly were the perfect combination for making sandwiches. They always made the children of the house happy during lunchtime. No one went hungry after eating a peanut butter and jelly sandwich in their house.

The jelly was happy with the peanut butter, but it always wondered what it would be like to make a sandwich with some of the other condiments in the refrigerator.

Then one day, the jelly had its chance to be with something new. The youngest daughter in the family decided to make her own sandwich for lunch. She got out the bread and placed the slices on her plate. She got out the jelly and spread it on one of the pieces of bread. Then she looked in the refrigerator for something besides peanut butter. She grabbed the ketchup and squirted it on the other slice of bread.

She smushed the slices of bread together to make a sandwich. The jelly was happy to be with something new, until it saw the look on the girl's face after she took a bite.

The girl screamed, "Yuck!" Then she spit the sandwich bite back onto her plate.

"Gross!" she said, with her tongue still sticking out.

The jelly felt ashamed. Peanut butter really was its perfect match. It now knew it no longer wanted to make sandwiches with anything else.

You shall not commit adultery.

THE BEAVERS' DAM

A husband and wife pair of beavers built a new dam together in a river with a strong current. They worked very hard and were nearly finished when the husband decided to go out looking for more sticks and supplies to finish their dam.

He left his wife and traveled upstream. Far up the river, he saw another beaver. She was a beautiful beaver. The most beautiful beaver he had ever seen. She was building her dam alone.

She was so beautiful that it made him nervous even to speak with her. "Could you use some help?" he asked her.

"Oh, yes, thank you!" she said.

The beaver worked diligently to help her for a very long time. She smiled at him often as they built the dam together, and this made him blush and smile.

When they finished, she thanked him, and he decided it was time to make his way back home. It was nearing the end of the day now. He had completely lost track of time.

He came back to the place where he and his wife had built their dam, but it was gone. The dam had washed away.

"Where have you been?" asked his wife.

The beaver was in shock. He had no answer.

"Where are the sticks and other supplies you went to get?" she asked him. "We needed them to finish the dam before it washed away!"

Still, the beaver had no answer. He was ashamed. He confessed to his wife where he had been all this time and told her about the beaver that he had helped upstream.

The wife was heartbroken. She couldn't believe her husband could do such a thing, and now the home they had built together was gone.

You shall not commit adultery.

THE SEVENTH COMMANDMENT

You shall not steal.

THE PRINCESSES' ACCESSORIES

There was a set of princess toys that had a lot of little items stored with them in their boxes. They had dozens of shoes and dresses and all sorts of things for them to use when their owner played with them. The princesses loved their accessories, but they were never satisfied with what they had. Every now and then, the owner would bring new accessories home for the princesses, but the dolls always wanted more.

One day, the mother in the house threw a pile of new accessories into the box with the princesses. Many of these accessories belonged to other toys. There were pots and pans. There were school items. There were even swords and weapons from the boys' toy box.

The princesses were so pleased. They had many new accessories to keep for themselves. They loved having more things, and they decided to hide these new items so they wouldn't get put back into their proper boxes.

The next day, the girl in the house played with the princesses and figurine animals together. The figurine animals had many accessories, too.

The girl heard her mother calling and had to leave the toys on the ground.

A princess doll with blonde hair saw that Mrs. Beaver was very sad.

"What's wrong?" asked the princess.

"I've lost my most prized possession," she said as she put her head into her hands.

"Well, can I help you find it? What does it look like?" asked the princess.

"It is Mr. Beaver's hat. It is all I have to remember him by. He was lost last year, and now his hat is lost, too! I'll never find it."

The princess felt awful. She remembered the hat and how she had hid it with the other accessories that were stored in the princess box by mistake.

"Mrs. Beaver, I am so sorry. The other princesses and I took the hat."

"What? Why would you do such a thing?" Mrs. Beaver asked.

"I have no good reason. I am so sorry. I will find the hat and everything else misplaced in our box and return it all to its rightful place."

The princesses spent the next many weeks of play returning the accessories they had hidden for themselves to the other toys.

You shall not steal.

THE BURIED TREASURE

On his walk home from work one day, a man took a shortcut through a farmer's field. Halfway through the field, he saw something shiny buried amid some stones. He walked over and removed the stones. There, he saw a shiny gold box filled with money. The man stood and looked to see if anyone was around. He saw that he was alone, so he took the golden box and hid it inside his coat.

He hurried to his home and hid the box in his backyard. The man checked back to make sure the box was there again and again throughout the day. He was very afraid that someone would steal his buried treasure as he had stolen it from the farmer.

He was so afraid that it would be found that he recovered the treasure box and buried it in a different spot. Then he was overcome with fear that the new spot would be too easily found, so he hid the box in another spot. He did this again and again, until one day he went to uncover his treasure and found that it wasn't there.

"NO!" he shouted and broke down in tears. From that day forward, he looked with suspicion and anger at anyone who walked near his home, accusing them in his heart of stealing the treasure.

All the while, the treasure stayed buried in his backyard. The man had moved it so many times, he had forgotten where he last buried it.

You shall not steal.

THE HUNGRY MICE

Two mice lived happily in the walls of a home. They had plenty of crumbs to eat from the people in the house, and they were too fast to be caught in any traps.

Then one day, the people brought home a cat from the pet store. The cat was cunning and liked to catch mice.

The mice were no longer able to roam freely in the house, and they had a much harder time finding food for themselves. Together, they could trick the cat and bring back some food, but never as much as they used to be able to find.

One day, one of the mice ate his companion's food during the day while she was sleeping. When the other mouse woke up, she was very angry with her friend and no longer wished to stay with him.

"If you had asked for some of the food, I gladly would have given it to you," she said. Then she left to look for another house where she could find more food.

The other mouse did not want to leave. He thought he could find enough food for himself without her.

The next day, he saw a piece of bread left under the dinner table. He scurried over to it and was about to bring it back to his home when the cat saw him and pounced on him.

There was no one there to help him. The cat captured and ate him.

You shall not steal.

THE CHEATER

There were new assigned seats in a class one day, and the teacher placed the top-performing student next to a boy who was struggling to do well on quizzes and tests. The boy was embarrassed about his grades, and he was afraid to let the well-performing girl know how poorly he was doing. It didn't help that he had a crush on her and wanted to impress her as much as he could.

The teacher administered the first quiz for the class in their new seats. The boy realized that the girl sitting nearby wasn't hiding her answers to the quiz very well. He could easily see what she wrote down.

On the first quiz, he only copied one answer from her. Then, when he didn't get caught, on the next quiz he copied a lot more. He continued to copy off of her without letting the teacher or the girl see him.

After school one day, the teacher pulled the boy aside. He was nervous that he might be caught. Instead, she praised him for doing so well. He had completely turned his grades around since moving into the new seat. She said she was proud of him.

The girl was waiting outside in the hall. She was smiling, too. She said she was so happy to hear how well he was doing. She was glad to be desk neighbors.

The boy couldn't take it anymore. He couldn't lie about what he had done. He turned back around and confessed all the cheating to the teacher. She was glad he confessed but quite disappointed in him for stealing the girl's answers.

The teacher notified his parents. She rearranged the seats in class the next day. She had to talk to the girl about hiding her answers. She changed the grades of all the quizzes he'd cheated on to failures but invited him to take them again for half credit.

The boy lost the respect and trust of the teacher, his parents, and especially the girl. She rarely ever spoke to him again.

You shall not steal.

THE MISSING SOCKS

The top drawer of a young girl's dresser always seemed to have a sock or two missing its match. This was because the dresser thought it would be funny to hide these socks and trick the little girl.

Day after day, a sock would be hidden by the dresser, leaving its match all alone. This went on for a very long time, until one day the dresser hid a bright pink sock with a unicorn on the side.

The next morning, when the girl woke up to get dressed, she searched the drawer for the missing sock.

"Oh, no! I can't find it!" she shouted, and tears began to fill up her eyes. "Mom! Help me!"

The girl's mother came up to her room to see what was wrong and found the girl in tears.

"What's wrong, honey?" her mother asked.

"I can't find one of my favorite socks—the one with the unicorn on it!" she cried.

"Well, then, maybe you should take better care of your things. C'mon, find another pair of socks and come downstairs for breakfast," said the mother.

The girl continued to cry. She sat down on the ground and bawled her eyes out.

The dresser suddenly realized how awful it was to take away the socks. The girl was sad that the socks were gone. They weren't lost. They were stolen.

When the little girl left the room, the dresser returned all of the missing socks to the drawer. When the girl returned, she saw her favorite socks and many others she had been missing.

"I found it, Mom!" she shouted with a smile, and from then on, the dresser kept good care of the socks kept in its drawers for the little girl.

You shall not steal.

THE EIGHTH COMMANDMENT

You shall not bear false witness against your neighbor.

THE FALSE FOX

There was a fox in the forest who wanted to be well liked among the other animals.

"I must get them to like me better than any other animal in the forest," he said to himself.

So he went through the forest spreading rumors and lies about the birds, the bears, and the groundhogs. He thought that this would make the other animals hate them and start to like him instead.

Then one day, the fox was caught in a hunter's trap.

Some birds flew by, and the fox shouted, "Birds, grab hold of this cage and lift it up into the air so I can escape!" They snickered at him and kept flying, because they had heard what he'd said about them.

A groundhog approached next, and the fox said, "Groundhog, dig me a hole so I can crawl under the cage and escape!" The groundhog had also heard the nasty rumors spread by the fox, so he turned to walk in a different direction.

Then a bear came by, and the fox said, "Bear, please pick up this cage and pull it off of me so I can run before the hunters return!" The bear knew what the fox had said about him, too, and continued to walk by without answering.

There was no one in the entire forest now to help the fox escape. The hunter returned, and the fox was captured.

You shall not bear false witness against your neighbor.

THE TRICKY CHICKENS

The chickens on a farm liked to play tricks on the other animals.

They pecked open the pigpen and let the pigs run amok through the fields. When the farmer came to see what had happened, the chickens clucked at the horse. The farmer blamed the horse and became angry with him instead of the chickens.

That night, the chickens continued to play tricks on the horse. They jumped on his back and pecked at his hindquarters until he got so angry he kicked the gate open and went running around the farm.

The farmer was even angrier than before at the horse, while the chickens laughed about their funny joke.

The next night, a fox snuck into the farm. The horse saw him heading toward the henhouse. He was about to alert the chickens, but he stopped and stayed quiet, remembering their mean tricks and false accusations.

The fox went into the henhouse, and with no one to warn them, all the chickens were eaten.

You shall not bear false witness against your neighbor.

THE HONEST GIRAFFE

The giraffe was the tallest animal on the savannah. He could see almost everything the other animals did. It was hard for them to hide from him, and everyone knew it.

To some of the animals, the giraffe's long neck looked strange. The hyena thought it was the funniest thing he had ever seen. He laughed a lot at all the animals, but he made fun of the giraffe more than anyone else.

One day, the zebra came up to the giraffe to talk about the hyena. "I am tired of listening to the hyena laugh at all the other animals. I have a plan to get rid of him, but I need your help," she said.

The plan was to bring the hyena to the lion, who was the ruler over the savannah, with the claim that the hyena had attacked the zebra. The zebra wanted the giraffe to say that he saw the hyena attack her.

So the next day, the zebra pretended to have a limp in her hind legs. She came with many other animals, including the giraffe, to speak with the lion. The lion summoned the hyena and listened carefully to the zebra's story.

The hyena laughed about the story and claimed that it couldn't be true.

"But the giraffe was the witness! Dear giraffe, tell them what you saw," said the zebra.

The giraffe looked at the zebra, then looked at the hyena. The hyena was holding in a laugh while looking at the giraffe's neck. This was the giraffe's chance to get rid of the hyena for good. All he had to do was tell the lion that the zebra's story was true. But the more he thought about it, the more he realized he couldn't bring himself to lie no matter how much he disliked the hyena.

"No," said the giraffe. "It isn't true. I didn't see the hyena hurt anyone. The zebra is lying."

"What? Of course he did! Look at me!" said the zebra.

The lion jumped toward the zebra and roared. The zebra jumped out of the way, clearly showing that her legs were not hurt.

"Zebra, you have lied, and for this you are banned from the savannah, never to return," said the lion. "Giraffe, thank you for speaking the truth."

The giraffe nodded his head with a long motion of his neck and returned to his home.

Thereafter, the hyena was grateful that the giraffe had defended him. He still wanted to laugh about the giraffe's neck, but he held it in and was as nice as he could be toward the giraffe.

You shall not bear false witness against your neighbor.

THE LYING LITTLE BROTHER

A young boy rode his bike through the neighborhood, wearing his favorite sunglasses. He was plotting the next trick to play on his big sister. What he loved to do most of all was get her into trouble when she did something wrong. He was wondering how he could get her into the biggest trouble of all when he had an idea. He and his sister were not allowed to play in their dad's office. What if he went in and made a mess, then blamed it on her?

He got home and hung his sunglasses on his t-shirt. Then he snuck into the house and into their father's office.

He took paper and pens out of the drawers and scribbled all over the paper. He knocked books off of the shelves. He moved the chairs and turned over picture frames. It was thoroughly a mess in there.

He went to his sister's room and said, "Dad wants to talk to you in his office. You're in trouble."

"For what?" she said.

"I don't know," said the boy.

As she went toward the office, the younger brother ran downstairs to his mom and said, "Mom, come see dad's office. It's a mess! Quick!"

They walked to the office and found his older sister standing there in the middle of the room.

"What are you doing in here, young lady?" asked their mother.

"Making a mess!" said the little brother with a smile.

"What, me? I didn't do this. Why would I make a mess in here? I know we're not even allowed in here," said the sister.

"Well, who did it then?" asked the mother. They both looked at the young boy, who was shaking his head in denial.

"He tried to frame me!" shouted the sister. "Look!" she pointed down at the ground beside their father's desk. There on the floor lay the boy's favorite sunglasses. They must have fallen off of his shirt.

The mother looked at the brother and said, "Well?"

"Yeah," he said looking down. "Yeah, it was me. I'm sorry."

"Clean it up and go to your room," she said. "You will need to write apology letters to your father for making a mess, to me for lying, and to your sister for trying to get her in trouble. Now, go!"

The little brother was filled with regret. He had made a big mistake, and now he was the one in trouble.

You shall not bear false witness against your neighbor.

THE GOSSIPING GIRL

There was a girl who always liked to be the center of attention. If she was with a group of girls, she wanted all of them to listen to the things she had to say. Sometimes she said things that weren't true to get more people to listen to her.

A boy in her class stopped coming to school one day. The teacher never explained to the class why he was absent, so the girl started to make up stories to get the attention of her classmates.

She told people that he was expelled from school. She shared all kinds of detailed lies about awful things he had done to get kicked out of school. They believed her, because the boy did get in trouble from time to time.

When the boy returned to school a week later, he had to answer a lot of questions about the false stories the girl had told about him.

He was very confused. None of it was true. There was a death in his family, so he had had to leave abruptly to travel for the funeral.

The girl felt awful for telling lies about the boy to get

her friends' attention. Her classmates never believed anything she said about anyone else again. She lost their trust and their respect.

You shall not bear false witness against your neighbor.

THE NINTH COMMANDMENT

You shall not covet your neighbor's wife.

THE THREE SWANS

A large group of swans lived in a small pond. Two of these swans were very much in love.

Among them lived a swan with an orange beak, and whenever he saw the two swans together, he felt very alone.

The orange-beaked swan longed to be in love like the other two swans. Because of this, he often found himself watching the female swan at a distance.

He watched her and watched her, and his desire for her grew and grew.

One day, the ducks caught him staring at the female and told her mate what they saw.

The mate came to the orange-beaked swan with all his other swan friends, and they banished him from the pond.

The orange-beaked swan flew away and had to find another place to live instead.

You shall not covet your neighbor's wife.

THE PRETEND HUSBAND

The prince and princess toys were in love. They rarely got into fights.

But one day, the owner played with the princess but left the prince in the toy box. Instead, she used the evil vampire as the princess's new husband. Even though the vampire was evil, he greatly desired the princess for himself and enjoyed being her pretend husband a little too much.

At night, the price started a fight with the princess. He was jealous of the vampire. When the vampire heard that the princess and prince were arguing, he came to comfort her, all the while planning to get rid of the prince.

The vampire made his plan. He was going to knock the toy box over and spill all the toys out in the morning. Then he would get his evil followers to help wrap the prince in rubber bands and throw him into the garbage.

Other toys overheard him telling his followers the plan and came to warn the prince. So the prince enlisted their help, along with all the other toys.

The next day, when the toy box fell, the prince and the other toys were ready for the attack. They had rubber bands of their own, and they tied up the evil toys, stopping them from disposing of the prince.

"Why would you do this?" the prince asked.

"The princess should be mine! I am a better husband than you ever could be," the vampire replied.

The princess came to the prince's side. The night before, he had asked for her forgiveness, and they were no longer angry with each other. She looked with sadness at the vampire, who was not even a very good pretend husband.

When the owner came in, she took the prince and princess out and played house with together once more.

As for the vampire, the rubber bands gave the owner's brother an idea. He picked up the toy and the rubber bands and said, "Rocket man!"

The boy catapulted the vampire off the back porch of the house and into the mud.

You shall not covet your neighbor's wife.

THE WEED AND THE FLOWERS

A red and a pink rose had intertwined themselves around each other so much that it seemed as though they were one flower.

There was a weed nearby, hidden beneath the shade of a barn. It longed to divide the two flowers and unite itself to the pink one.

The weed grew and grew and began to wrap itself around the pink rose. Round and round it grew, trying to separate it from the red rose. The roses were very afraid of losing each other. They feared that they would be completely pushed apart.

Meanwhile, the gardener came to tend the flowers. She saw the weed and untangled it from the flowers and pulled out the root hidden below the barn. She threw it in the fire pit to be burned later that day.

You shall not covet your neighbor's wife.

THE TENNIS SHOE

A woman had a closet full of shoes of many different kinds. The shoes all shared one thing in common: they wanted to be worn and taken out into the world.

Most of the shoes were happy to be worn no matter what the woman did. There was a tennis shoe, however, that got tired of only being worn to go running through the neighborhood. It wished it could go out on adventures like the rain boots. It loved to listen to the boots tell their stories of splashing in puddles, pouring rain, and sticky mud. The tennis shoe was hardly ever splashed in mud or puddles.

The tennis shoe imagined what it would be like to go out into the world with one of the rain boots instead of its matching tennis shoe. It imagined all the fun adventures it could have together with the rain boots.

Because of this, it stopped talking about the fun running adventures with its partner. It dreamed instead of being with a rain boot. It looked at its own partner, which had fraying threads and worn down soles, with disappointment. The rain boots seemed so new. The other tennis shoe seemed so old and was even beginning to fall apart.

The two shoes drifted apart and rarely ever spoke to one another anymore.

Then one day, the woman took the tennis shoes off the shelf and into the garage near the garden tools. Now she only wore them to do yard work. The tennis shoes got muddy and wet. They had a lot to talk about in the garage. They had many new adventures, and they were happy to be worn in such new and exciting ways.

Soon the tennis shoe began to feel remorse for so many lost days wishing it was with a rain boot instead. It apologized to its partner tennis shoe for dreaming about being with another shoe.

The shoes had many wonderful memories of running and exercising in the past, and now they got to share a whole new set of memories. The tennis shoe was pleased and knew it didn't want to share these memories with any other shoe in the world anymore.

You shall not covet your neighbor's wife.

THE OLD WOLVES

A pair of wolves lived together as husband and wife for many years. In the beginning of their relationship, they were very much in love. They spent every moment together and loved to roam the forest.

The husband, though, was growing old and slow. He didn't hunt as much as he used to. Instead, he enjoyed resting in the sun on a cool day or in the shade on a hot day.

On one summer morning, a bear happened to come across the den where these two wolves were sleeping. He was surprised, and he attacked because he was afraid that the wolves might attack him. But the husband wolf didn't fight back. He cowered away in fear that he wasn't fast enough to fend off the bear.

Another wolf nearby heard the commotion. He was young and strong. He came to the aid of the pair of wolves and fought the bear. The battle didn't last long. The bear didn't really want a fight, so he ran off into the forest.

The wife looked on their hero in awe. She was embarrassed by her husband. He was a disappointment.

In the days that followed, the wife dreamed about that

day that the young wolf came to save them. She imagined what life would be like if she were with him instead of her husband. She pictured herself going on adventures with the young wolf, just as she had done with her husband all those years ago.

Her husband, meanwhile, felt ashamed for his cowardice. He spent more and more time lounging rather than hunting. He constantly compared himself to the courageous wolf and felt bad about what he had become.

The pair never talked about that day with the bear. They hid their thoughts and dreams about other wolves and other lives, and this made them feel even farther apart. The more they thought about the young, courageous wolf, the sadder they were about their lives together. Their love slowly faded away, leaving them both unhappy and lonely.

You shall not covet your neighbor's wife.

THE TENTH COMMANDMENT

You shall not covet your neighbor's goods.

THE BETTER BIKE

A young boy moved into a new neighborhood and went out to ride his bike. On the ride, he saw the other neighborhood boys' bikes parked in their garages or lying on the sidewalks. There were big black bikes and shiny silver bikes. There were bikes with electric motors and bikes with fancy seats.

Some other boys were riding their bikes so fast that they nearly ran into him from behind. "Look out!" they yelled as they passed by.

The boy looked at his bike with sadness and wished he had one of the other boys' bikes.

He was turning to ride home when he noticed the coolest bike he had ever seen. He couldn't keep his eyes off it, and he pedaled faster and faster to get a better look.

He was pedaling hard but not watching where he was going. He ran his bike right into a mailbox.

The boy wasn't hurt badly, but his bike was irreparably damaged. His parents made him sell the undamaged parts of the bike to help their neighbor pay for a new mailbox. Now when he looked at the other boys riding their bikes, he only wished he had his old bike back so that he could ride with them.

You shall not covet your neighbor's goods.

THE COMPUTER AND THE STICKERS

The desktop computer in a young girl's room had been there for years. She used it almost every day to talk to her friends, finish her homework, and listen to music.

As the girl got older, however, she started to bring home newer and smaller devices. Now, she used a tablet every day and hardly ever touched that old computer anymore.

The computer was sad and missed helping the girl. More than that, though, it wished it had some of the decorative stickers that she put on the tablet.

There were new stickers all the time, with beautiful images and designs. She made that tablet look so new and fresh with each new sticker.

The only sticker on the computer was a partially ripped off sticker that the girl had gotten for free at the grocery store. She hadn't even scraped off the sticky residue from the part that she ripped off.

One day, the girl plugged the tablet into the computer to charge and transfer photos to the computer. She set the tablet on top of the computer and left the room as the files transferred.

The tablet's stickers were now touching the top of the computer. This just made the computer even more sad, and then it began to be angry.

Then it had an idea. What if it got hot enough to melt the stickers so that the designs would burn onto it, as well?

The computer turned off its fan and got hotter and hotter. It could feel the stickers starting to melt onto it.

Then something went wrong. Something inside burned out, and everything went dark. The computer shut down.

A long time later, the computer turned on again. It was fixed, but it was in a different place. It was surrounded by other old computers. Some of them had half-ripped stickers, too.

The girl, however, was gone. She must have gotten rid of the computer and sold it to be refurbished. The computer never saw her again.

You shall not covet your neighbor's goods.

THE COVETOUS CANDLEMAKER

A candlemaker opened his first store in the town square, but very few people came to buy from him. He would stand outside of his shop, looking at the other shopkeepers' long lines and many customers.

"If only I had the number of customers that my neighbors have," he said to himself.

He was most jealous of the jewelry store on the other side of town. Every time he walked by their shop, the lines were long and the people were happy. He grew tired of his boring candles and longed to sell something glamorous like jewelry instead. So he sold off his candles to another shopkeeper and started a jewelry store.

Soon after, a great magician cast a spell of darkness throughout the land. There was no daylight for weeks and weeks. People began selling everything they had, even their jewelry, to buy candles to light up their homes.

By now, the candlemaker had no candles to sell and no money left to buy the supplies he needed to make candles for the many people who needed them.

You shall not covet your neighbor's goods.

THE DEFENSELESS RABBITS

Two rabbits hopped through the forest. One rabbit began to complain along the way. He was angry with God because rabbits are given so little to defend themselves.

"Look at the turtle," he said. "The turtle has a shell to protect himself from enemies."

"Yes, or think of the porcupine," his friend added. "He has a back full of spikes as his defense."

"Or the skunk," the first rabbit went on. "He can spray that awful smell on his attackers."

They continued to give example after example of other animals that had better defenses than them, when suddenly, they heard a noise. It was a human hunter with a gun, ready to kill any animal he saw.

The rabbits froze when they saw him. Then, when he came close, they scrambled away with such speed that the hunter didn't even see them.

They slowed down a safe distance away. Panting and exhausted, they spoke to one another again.

"Maybe I was wrong," said the first rabbit. "Maybe we have been given good gifts to defend ourselves."

"You're right," said his friend. "Imagine if we were a turtle or a porcupine or a skunk. The hunter would have shot those slow creatures, while we were able to run away."

You shall not covet your neighbor's goods.

THE GAMER

There was a boy that loved to play video games. He played games every night after finishing his homework and as much as he could on the weekends.

At school, the other kids talked about their new video games, too. A friend of his bragged about his latest new game. The boy wished he had the game, too, so he begged his mom to buy it for him.

After much begging, she finally gave in and bought the game for him. He played every day for the next week.

But another friend was playing a different game. The boy wanted this game, too. He begged his mom nonstop until finally she bought him the other game, as well.

"This is the last game for a long time, okay?" she told him.

But the next week, every kid in school was talking about a new, even better video game craze. It seemed like everyone owned it and everyone was playing it.

The boy went to his mother to ask for the game. "Please! It is the best game ever, and the other kids won't stop talking about it," he pleaded.

"No, I just bought you two new games. Play those. I'm not buying another one," she said.

He begged for days, but she didn't relent. Instead, he could only play his other games, which were now old news, and never got to join in the fun of the greatest new game that all the other kids in school were talking about.

You shall not covet your neighbor's goods.

ABOUT THE AUTHOR

Jared Dees is the creator of TheReligionTeacher.com, a popular website that provides practical resources and teaching strategies to religious educators. A respected graduate of the Alliance for Catholic Education (ACE) program at the University of Notre Dame, Dees holds master's degrees in education and theology, both from Notre Dame. He frequently gives keynote addresses and leads workshops at conferences, church events, and school in-services throughout the year on a variety of topics. He lives near South Bend, Indiana, with his wife and children.

Learn more about Jared's books, speaking events, and other projects at jareddees.com.

ALSO BY JARED DEES

Beatitales: 80 Fables about the Beatitudes for Children

31 Days to Becoming a Better Religious Educator

To Heal, Proclaim, and Teach

Praying the Angelus

Christ in the Classroom

FORMATIVE FICTION

Jared Dees writes stories that help kids find confidence, character, and a relationship with Christ.

In the ***Formative Fiction Friday Newsletter,*** you will receive a new fable, short story, or serialized children's book by email every week that you can read or share with your children to help them learn life's most important lessons.

Learn more at:

jareddees.com/formativefiction

Made in the USA
Columbia, SC
01 June 2021